W9-AVK-480

The Sanyasin's First Day

by Ned Shank
illustrated by Catherine Stock

Marshall Cavendish New York

Marshall Cavendish, 99 White Plains Road, Tarrytown, NY 10591
Library of Congress Cataloging-in-Publication Data
Shank, Ned.
The sanyasin's first day / by Ned Shank ; illustrated by Catherine Stock. p. cm.
Summary: Describes the first day of work for several different people including a holy man, a farmer, a plumber, and a policeman, many of whom end up interacting with one another in the course of the day.
ISBN 0-7614-5055-6
[1. India—Juvenile fiction. 2. India—Fiction. 3. Occupations—Fiction.] I. Stock, Catherine, ill. II. Title.
PZ7.S52842San 1998 98-50740 CIP AC
Printed in Italy. First edition
6 5 4 3 2 1

With love to my parents,
Georgene and Wesley Shank,
who gave me my first day.
— N. S.

For Ajith, Ammu, Chandran, Chanu, Nirmala
Ranjit, Sabra, Vanessa and Victoria — Nani
—C. S.

Elite
TAILORS

It was the sanyasin's first day.

He sat in the shade of a tree beside the busy road with his walking stick, dressed in his brand-new orange cloth. He had given away everything he owned to lead the holy life of a sanyasin, to do nothing but pray, and walk from town to town dressed in orange, begging for just enough rice to fill his bowl.

GREENFIELD
FARM PRODUCE
BRITANNI
BUS STOP
KL01
E946

Women walked past him, their long, black braids with flowers tucked into the ends swinging at the waists of their brightly-colored saris. Men in white shirts and dhotis went by, carrying large black umbrellas opened over their heads against the hot sun. Children carrying schoolbooks looked at him and giggled, pushing against each other and running off, their sandals flip-flopping in the dusty road. A dog came up and sniffed his empty bowl.

"Oh, please," he prayed, "let someone put rice in my bowl to give me something to eat."

It was the plumber's first day.

She came to work in her plumber's overalls, with her wrenches and screwdrivers and pipe-fitting tools all in a red metal toolbox. She'd taken all the plumbing classes, passed her exams, and worked as an apprentice to a master plumber to learn her trade. Today she had her first job, to install a new kitchen sink. She took a deep breath and knocked on Mrs. Krishnan's door.

"Oh, please," she thought, "let me plumb her sink well, with no leaks and all the pipe joints tight."

dul kader
OLD ARTICLES
17

It was the traffic policeman's first day.

He stood on the center island stand that morning, in the middle of the busy intersection in the center of the town, eyeing the honking taxis and beeping three-wheeled open autorickshaws and rumbling paint-decorated lorries and bicycles with their bells clanging and the oxcarts from the country all around him.

He was dressed in his official uniform, with a black-brimmed cap pulled down over his eyes, crisply-ironed khaki shortsleeved shirt with braid looping over the right shoulder, uniform shorts with military buckled belt, long brown woolen socks and official shiny heavy brown boots. His hands were in white gloves, and a silvery metal whistle on a white cord hung in his mouth.

He'd trained blowing his whistle in school and moving his gloved hands to guide traffic smoothly and with authority. At night he'd practiced and practiced at home in front of the mirror. Now the lorries and cars and autorickshaws and bicycles and oxcarts waited noisily all around for him to guide them through the intersection.

"Oh, please," he whispered to himself, "let me direct the traffic safely and quickly."

A ABBAS
LUCKY CENTRE
Coca-Co
ST MARYS
HMI METALS
SELVANATHER
PUBLIC CARRIER
POX
3669
LIONS
7

It was the farmer's first day.

She sat at the front of the wooden two-wheeled oxcart, wearing a dark cotton sari with her change purse tucked safely in the folds of cloth at her waist. She held the reins leading to the two oxen she'd hitched to the cart, their broad muscular backs to her and their tall gracefully curving horns arching upwards. For this auspicious day, she'd painted their horns blue and hung garlands of flowers from them to rings in their noses. A small white bird perched on one of the oxen's

shoulders, looking for pesky bugs. Piled behind her were sacks of rice from her fields.

Her father had left yesterday morning to move in with her brother and his family in the city. She had worked alongside him all year planting and growing the slender green rice plants in the watery paddies, harvesting them at the end of the growing season. Now he'd left them all to her, and she was taking the first load to sell at the granary in the town.

"Oh, please," she called out to the oxen, "let me get a good price for the grain."

Gitchee
Fathima

"Two blocks straight ahead, then turn right at the statue of Gandhi," said the traffic policeman to the farmer in her oxcart. "That is where you can sell your rice. Wait while I hold up traffic to let you cross." He whistled and gestured with his white-gloved hands to make everyone stop while she slowly drove her team across the intersection.

"I am walking to the market to buy some food while you finish working," said Mrs. Krishnan to the plumber crouched below the new sink, cutting the water pipes. "Then I will cook us both some lunch, and take some to my son Gopi Nathan at his school."

Just as she passed the statue of Gandhi she saw the farmer in her oxcart. "Miss, miss," cried out Mrs. Krishnan, "let me buy some rice!"

"What is all this?" thought the farmer as she looked down the long tree-covered road lined on each side with vendors of all kinds. There were stalls filled with oranges, coconuts, limes, chilies, mangoes, and pineapples. Others sold sweet candies and chewing gum and cookies and chocolate bars; some had stacks of shiny round metal water-vessels and brightly-colored plastic buckets and stainless steel ladles and spatulas and rice cookers. One man had a table filled with brass oil

lamps of every size. A moving cart sold cold sodas and hot coffee and tea, all in thick glasses.

But she saw no one selling rice. "I'd asked for directions to the granary to sell all my bags of rice, but perhaps I will do better here," she thought. She pulled over to the side and found some newspaper and string.

"Yes, yes," she said to Mrs. Krishnan who was still waiting by her cart. "I can sell you a kilo of rice. But we'll have to guess at the weight since I have no scale." And she made a cone from a piece of newspaper, poured in the rice to make it full and tied it up with the string.

"Pay me what you think it is worth," said the farmer, and the woman did. A line quickly formed since she had the only rice there, and word spread of her unusual way of doing business.

"There, now," said the plumber to herself, rubbing her hands together, "that should do it!" The sink was installed and all the pipes connected. Not a pipe was leaking, and she began to put away her tools and figure her bill.

Mrs. Krishnan came in the door with her packages and looked at the plumber with one eyebrow raised questioningly. "Yes, you may use the sink now," the plumber told her proudly.

The woman put some of the rice in a pot and put it under the new faucet.

"SWOOOOSSSHHH!!" went the water from the faucet, quickly filling up the pot.

"What happened?" cried Mrs. Krishnan.

"Too much pressure! I'll adjust the valve underneath. But is that too much water for your rice?" asked the plumber.

"No," said Mrs. Krishnan, shaking water from her hands, "it's no problem. I got too much anyway at the market." And she poured in the rest of the rice to cook.

After lunch, Mrs. Krishnan paid the bill and the plumber walked home.
"I'm so happy," thought the plumber, "to have done a good job!"

Mrs. Krishnan put some of the cooked rice and the rest of the lunch into a small stainless steel tiffin, and then added another tin with some of the extra rice. She walked to Gopi Nathan's school and gave her son his lunch.

కుంగదీసిన
TATA
SOUND
HORN

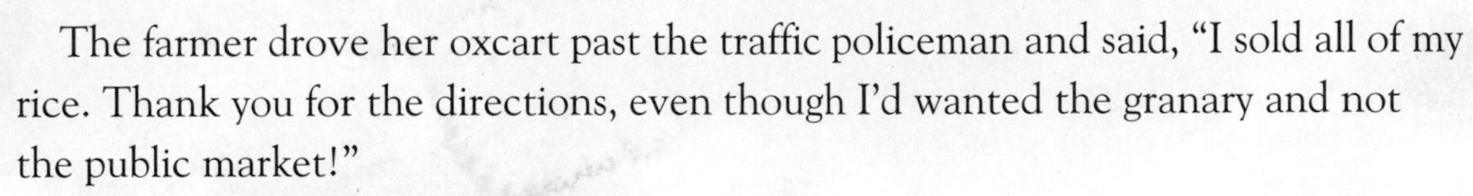

The farmer drove her oxcart past the traffic policeman and said, "I sold all of my rice. Thank you for the directions, even though I'd wanted the granary and not the public market!"

"You're welcome," he said, "and I'm glad it turned out all right." And he blew his whistle to stop traffic until she crossed.

"I'm so happy," the farmer called out to her oxen, "for getting a good price for my grain!"

Later that afternoon, the traffic policeman blew his whistle loudly and held up his gloved hands to stop traffic in all directions. Two long lines of school children going home for the day carrying their schoolbooks were crossing the street.

“How was your first day?” asked Sergeant Rama when he came to take over for the next shift.

“Not bad,” said the traffic policeman. “No accidents, no traffic jams.”

“But truly,” he said to himself as he walked away, “I’m so happy, to have directed traffic safely and quickly all day.”

"Are you really a sanyasin?" asked Gopi Nathan, holding his schoolbooks and luncheon tins, of the orange-clothed man sitting under the tree by the side of the dusty road with his walking stick and empty wooden bowl.

"Yes," said the sanyasin. "I really am."

The boy emptied a tin of rice into the wooden bowl. "My mother made me extra; I promise I have not touched it." It was just enough to fill the bowl, and the boy left.

BUS
STOP
MAFAFLAL

"Thank You," thought the sanyasin as he went to sleep at the end of his first day. "Thank You, for answering my prayer."